This book belongs to:

....

....

Love you Chloe & Ben.
It is a long time since your first day of school,
but our love for you gets bigger everyday.
Mum & Dad

A NEW BURLINGTON BOOK

Editor: Sophie Hallam
Designer: Michael Henson

© 2015 Quarto Publishing plc

This edition first published in 2018 by QED Publishing,
an imprint of The Quarto Group.
The Old Brewery, 6 Blundell Street
London N7 9BH, United Kingdom.
T (0)20 7700 6700 F (0)20 7700 8066
www.QuartoKnows.com

A catalogue record for this book is available from
the British Library.

ISBN 978 1 78493 485 9

Manufactured in Guangdong, China TT042018

9 8 7 6 5 4 3 2

Little Hedgehog's BIG Day

Daniel and Heidi Howarth

NEW BURLINGTON

"Only a few days
to go until you
start big school!"
said Mum.

Little Hedgehog smiled. He knew Mum was
excited so he pretended he was too...

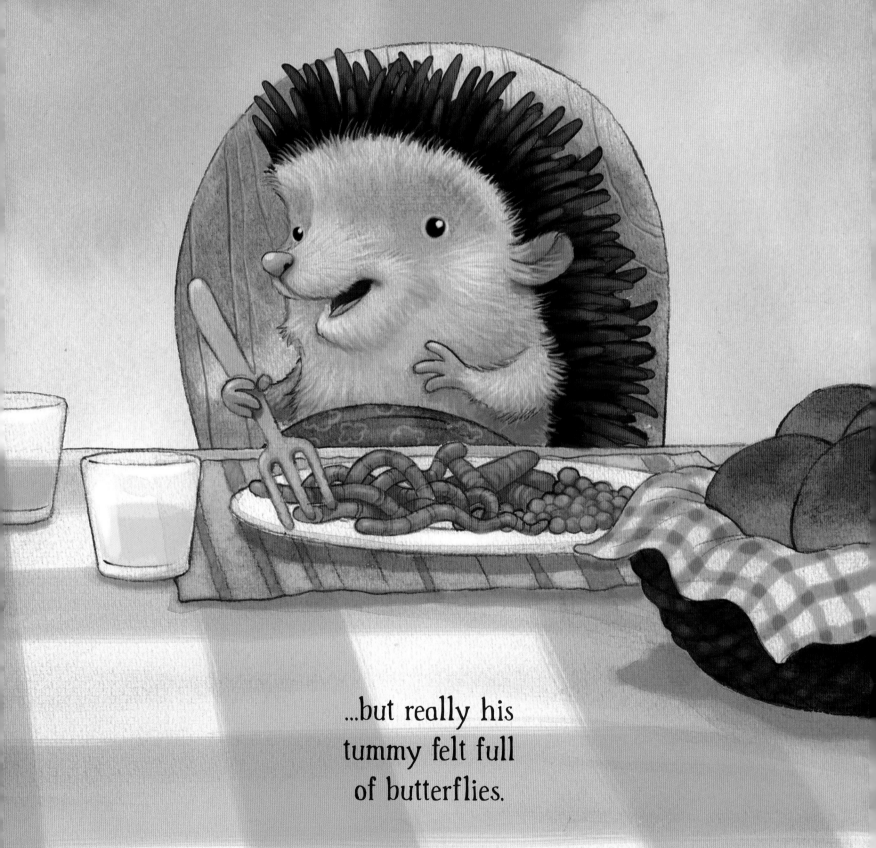

...but really his
tummy felt full
of butterflies.

That night Little Hedgehog was too worried to sleep...

He kept thinking about how big BIG SCHOOL would be.

Would there be a **big** table?

Would there be a **big** chair?

Would there be a **big** teacher?!

In the morning he knew
what he needed to do...

He had to get big,

really BIG!

But how?

"Exercise!"
said Rabbit.

"I bounce at least a hundred times a day.
It makes me strong and my legs long."

Rabbit stretched out his big bunny leg and Little Hedgehog compared it to his own. His looked tiny.

"Oh and I eat carrots... lots and lots of carrots," Rabbit said before bouncing away.

"Oh no," said Squirrel, "jumping makes you big. And eating nuts... lots and lots of nuts."

"They make me strong!" he said, flexing his muscles.

"See?" He jumped up quickly and dangled from a branch.

Little Hedgehog jumped but there was no way he could reach!

"Stretching," yawned Badger. "I get bigger every time I stretch."

Little Hedgehog stretched
next to Badger but it just
made him feel even smaller.

So Little Hedgehog tried to

bounce like Rabbit...

..*jump* like Squirrel...

..and *stretch* like Badger.

But he **still** didn't feel any bigger.

"What are you doing?"
asked Ant.

"I need to be **big**,"
cried Little Hedgehog,
"for **big** school!"

"Why?" said Ant. "I'm small but
I can still do **lots** of things!"

When he got home,
Little Hedgehog ran
to find his mum.

"Do you think I am ready for big
school?" he asked her.

"Well," she replied
thoughtfully,
"let's have a look."

She took down a photo
album from the shelf.

Inside were lots of photos of Little Hedgehog.

"Just look at all the things you have
done already," said Mum proudly.

Then Mum showed him an old picture
of a little hedgehog, with a school cap
and a shiny satchel.

"Goodness, that was my first day at school!"
said Dad from the doorway.

On the first day of school, Little Hedgehog was all ready to go.

"I look just like you, Dad!"
he said, smiling.

Little Hedgehog went to school
and it wasn't so big after all!

He took out his book and was just
practising his letters when...

"Wow," said Badger. "Can you show us?" they all asked together.

"Of course I can," he smiled. "I can do lots of things!"

Next steps

Look at the cover of the book together. What is Little Hedgehog wearing? Do the children remember their first day at school, or are they starting school very soon?

Anything new can be a little bit scary. Everyone has felt 'butterflies' in their tummy when faced with a new place, new people or a new experience. Take this opportunity to talk to the children about school. Were they excited to be going? Or nervous, like Little Hedgehog? What were they excited or worried about?

Talk about the story. Little Hedgehog is worried – what does he try and do to solve his worries? What makes Little Hedgehog feel better in the end?

Little Hedgehog realizes all the things he can do which make him feel really big inside. What talents do the children have? What do they like to do?

In the story, Little Hedgehog is shown a book of photographs. Have the children ever seen pictures of themselves or their parents when they were younger? Have they ever seen any very old photographs of their families? If you can, print out some photos to help the children make their own photo album or draw a family tree.